Fantasy

By

RHAYNE

Fantasy

Table of Contents

Prologue

7 Months Earlier

Chloe

I was on top of the world. Everything was great with school, work, and my love life. Devin, my new boyfriend, and I had been dating for six months when I decided it was time for my friends to meet him.

The perfect opportunity came when Sonya, my roommate, and I invited friends over for a fourth of July barbecue. Everyone got along great, which made an enjoyable evening.

After all the guests had left, Devin, Destini, my BFF, and AJ- Devin's friend, stayed behind, and we continued our own little party.

We were all pretty wasted, so I suggested that the three of them stay overnight.

"Destini, you can bump with me if you like, and AJ, you can sleep on the sofa." Sonya offered.

"Or I can bump with you, and Destini can get the sofa bed." AJ winked.

"Not gonna happen," Sonya retorted.

"That's cool," Destini said.

"Well, since that's settled, who wants to join me for a little smoke?" AJ asked, taking a joint out of his shirt pocket.

"I don't think so." I waved my index finger back and forth. "Not in here."

"Chloe, don't be such a party pooper," Sonya replied, sitting next to AJ. "Man, light it up."

"I'm in, too," Destini said, as she sat on the other side of AJ.

"Well, Devin and I will be in my room."

I started walking down the hallway but stopped when I noticed Devin wasn't following me. I turned around, only to find him standing in the same spot.

"Devin, don't tell me you smoke, too."

It was more of a statement than a question.

"No, I don't smoke, but I don't want to be shut up in the bedroom either."

"You two can sit here on the sofa, and we will go to the table." Sonya stood and went over to the dining room table. Destini and AJ followed behind her.

"It doesn't matter, Sonya, we are still going to smell it." I retorted.

Our apartment was a living room-dining room combo. So, it didn't matter where they moved regarding that space.

"Babe, just let them have their fun. It's only one joint. They will be done in no time," Devin said.

"It doesn't matter if it's one joint or ten joints. I don't want it in here. But since I'm outvoted, have your fun. I'm going to my room."

I grabbed the half a bottle of crown apple off the kitchen counter and headed down the hallway. Just as I was polishing off the last bit of crown, I heard noises. I stood to see what was going on but fell back on the bed. I stood again, this time holding on to the end table for balance. I staggered my way down the hall. When I entered the living room, I couldn't believe my eyes. AJ, Destini, and Sonya were on the couch having a ménage a trios. Devin, on the other hand, was standing there enjoying their sexcapade.

Devin grabbed me by the arm and pulled me next to him.

"What in the world?"

"I know." He grinned. "But you know, babe, it's kind of hot. Got a brother wanting to join in."

"Nope." I shook my head.

He kissed me on the neck. "Please babe, do this for me."

He put his hand in my shorts and began teasing my girlie spot. Like a selfish friend, she betrayed me and began to throb. The more he stroked her, the more she ached for his attention. He slid his finger inside of me, and I gasped. He looked into my eyes and kissed me passionately.

"Please," he said after breaking the kiss.

"Let's take it to the bedroom." I took his hand and led the way.

Everything inside of me said I was making a big mistake, but I went along anyway.

When we entered the bedroom, Destini kissed me on the mouth, then pulled my shirt over my head and unfastened my bra.

Standing behind me, Sonya kissed my neck and unfastened my shorts. She slowly pulled them down and started playing in my bush.

Destini took one of my nipples in her mouth and teased it with her tongue, causing my inner core to tingle. Destini stopped long enough to guide me to the bed. After I laid down, Sonya spread my legs and dipped her tongue in my honey cup. I gasped, then let out a moan. She glided her tongue up to my bud and flicked it, before covering it with her warm mouth. I looked over at Devin. He and AJ were standing back, enjoying the show. I waved my hand for them to join us, and that's when everything went wrong.

Destini quickly took Devin in her mouth. Before I could protest, Sonya had me jerking with pleasure.

It appeared, the more AJ gave it to her, the better she gave it to me. I was lost in drunken ecstasy, and nothing else mattered at that moment.

I will admit it was a mind-blowing experience. Still, that decision was the worst one I could have ever made because it changed our lives forever.

Part One:
Reflection

Chloe

Destini and I met in the summer of my freshman year in college. I was a cashier in the school cafeteria. One day while at work, I saw Destini sitting alone. She must have really been enjoying the book she was reading because she didn't appear to be bothered by the noise around her. When lunchtime was almost over, I decided to get a head start on wiping off the tables. I walked over to the table next to where she was sitting, and she struck up a conversation with me.

"Hi," she said.

I looked around to see who she was talking to because girls like her usually didn't speak to girls like me.

She chuckled. "I'm speaking to you."

"Oh, hi," I said, taken aback. As I said, girls like her don't usually talk to me.

"Do you like working here in the cafeteria?"

"Not really, but hey, it keeps money in my pocket," I shrugged.

"Well, what if I tell you, I know how you can make more money than you are making here and you don't have to work as hard."

I raised a brow. "What kind of work is it?"

Destini held her hand up. "Don't worry. It's legal." She pulled a chair out from the table. "Have a seat."

"I can't. I'm still on the clock. Can I call you later?"

"Sure, that will be great."

I pulled my cell phone out of my apron. "Okay, give me your number."

"It is 555-5432."

"Got it. What's a good time to call you?"

"Eight o'clock is good." She stood up and pushed her chair under the table. "I will be waiting for that call." She smiled and walked away.

I called out behind her. "Hey, what's your name?"

"Destini," she said as she disappeared on the other side of the door.

After work, I went by the cleaners to pick up my dress for an all-white party. I was invited to by my psychology professor, Trevor Dents.

Each year, he invited those of us who had a 3.5 or above average in his class, to his annual fraternity banquet. The GBM's (Great Black Men) are the bomb. They do a lot of positive things in the community, like after school tutoring and mentoring young black boys, so they can grow up to be GBM's.

When I arrived home, my roommate, Sonya, was watching television. Sonya Bari and I have been roommates since our freshman year in college. Our relationship has grown over the past four years, and I can honestly say without a shadow of a doubt that she is my best friend, unlike Destini, but that's another story.

"Hi," I said, struggling to get through the door with books in one hand and my dress in the other.

"Hi." Sonya came over and held the door for me.

"Thank you."

"No problem." She sat back down and continued watching her program.

"Did I get any mail?"

"No, but some guy has been calling you all day."

"Did he leave a name?"

"No. He kept saying he would call you back."

"He's probably a telemarketer."

I walked to my bedroom, threw the books on the bed, and hung my dress in the closet.

I walked back into the living room. "So, what do you feel like having for dinner?" Sonya and I took turns cooking, and it was my day to prepare our meal.

"What about some sloppy joes?"

"Sounds good. I'll check to see if we have all of the ingredients."

"We do. I stopped by the store and got what we didn't have."

"Awesome. Well, I'm going to take a shower before I get started."

I walked into my bedroom and gathered some clothes, a washcloth, and a towel then headed for the bathroom. After I got undressed, I stood in the mirror and gave myself a look over. My honey brown skin was silky smooth like a baby, and my perfect size 34c breasts were full and perky. I did a half turn to get a look at my plump apple bottom and smiled, then broke into a twerk, before getting into the shower.

When I returned to the kitchen, Sonya joined me.

"Hey, that guy called again while you were in the shower," she said, taking the ground beef out of the refrigerator and sitting it on the counter.

"What did he say?"

"Nothing, he just hung up the phone. Are you in some kind of trouble?"

"No, I'm not in any trouble."

"Well, aren't you a little curious about what he could want with you?"

"Not really. Did his number show up on the caller ID?"

"Nope. It shows private."

"Well, it can't be too important." I shrugged.

"You would think since he's called so many times, he would leave his number."

"I concur," she said, walking back into the living room.

I finished cooking and made our sandwiches. Sonya grabbed the chips out of the pantry, and we sat in the living room watching NCIS while eating our dinner. During one of the commercials, I told her about my conversation with Destini. She didn't have much to say; however, she was just as curious about the job as I was.

At eight o'clock on the dot, I called Destini.

"Hello."

"Hello, Destini?" I asked.

"Yes."

"This is Chloe." I paused. "We met in the cafeteria."

"Hi, Chloe. I'm glad you called."

"Yeah, well, you have me curious about this job offer."

"Like I told you, it's legal."

"What is it, and what do I have to do?"

"Right to the point, I see." She chuckled.

"Well, it's a call center position. All you would have to do is answer the phone."

"Really? I can do that."

"Exactly."

"So, how much does it pay?"

"Well, that can be a little tricky, because you are strictly on commission."

"Okay, explain how this is going to make me more money. Because my pay is guaranteed as long as I work the hours."

"You are guaranteed to make money, the moment you pick up the phone," she said reassuringly.

"So, what am I selling?"

"Fantasy."

"Fantasy. What is Fantasy, some kind of cologne or something?"

Destini laughed.

"No, girl, it's just what I said, fantasy." She sighed.

"Okay, I need you to stop beating around the bush and tell me what this job entails," I said with sternness to let her know I didn't have time for games.

"Alright, this is what it is. Our call center is named Fantasy. We are a phone sex center. When customers call, both men and women, we help them carry out their sexual desires over the telephone."

"Will I be on camera?"

"Nope, all they would know about you is what you tell them. They will know your voice and that you are the one assisting them with their fantasy. We ask that you don't give the customers your name, but you will need to come up with a name, preferably something sexy."

"Hmmm, sounds interesting, but I don't know. Let me think about it, and I will get back to you."

"I tell you what, come by tomorrow and I will show you first-hand what we do."

"Okay."

"Is four o'clock okay with you?" "Yes, that's perfect."

"Great. We are located at 123 Leonix Way. I'll see you at four," she said before ending the call.

"You have reached your destination. 123 Leonix Way will be on your right." The voice on the navigation system announced.

I pulled into the driveway of a two-story brick home. The house was lovely, but the yard left a little to be desired. The grass needed to be cut, and the leaves that had fallen from the large magnolia tree in the front yard needed to be raked. I walked up to the house and pushed the doorbell.

"Who is it?" The voice from the other side

of the door asked.

"I'm Chloe. I'm here to see Destini." I replied.

The door opened. "Hi, I'm Anna. Come in." She stepped aside for me to enter.

Anna was Asian and African American descent. She was around five foot four and petite. Her burgundy hair was pulled back in a ponytail, and she wore black-rimmed eyeglasses that went very well with her face.

"Destini will be down in a minute," she said as she led me to the entertainment room in the back of the house.

I must say, the inside of the house was no reflection of the outside. The foyer and living areas were painted a soft gray. The white three-piece furniture set in the living room was accentuated with red and zebra-striped pillows on the sofa and loveseat. There was walnut wood flooring throughout each room, and the beautiful art pieces that adorned the walls were absolutely stunning.

When we got to the entertainment room, it was just the opposite. It was painted terracotta, which is quite similar to an orange but has a softer color tone. The room had a large middle brown sectional that reclined on each end. On the wall, in front of the sectional couch, was a large flat-screen television. To the left, where what could have been a dining area, was a pool table, and behind it was a small kitchenette that served as a bar.

Anna introduced me to the two young men sitting on the couch. They were watching a football game and didn't seem to notice when we entered the room.

"Chloe, this is my boyfriend Ty, short for Tyson," she said, pointing at him. He was gorgeous. He had caramel skin and beautiful green eyes.

"And this is Jeff, our roommate."

Jeff was Caucasian, he looked like a young Channing Tatum without all the muscles, yet still equally attractive.

"Nice to meet you." I exchanged a handshake with both of them.

"Have a seat." Anna sat next to Ty, and I sat next to her.

"So, I hear you are interested in joining the team," she smiled, and for the first time since I arrived, I noticed her braces.

"Yes, does the job pay well?"

"Oh, yes, honey, you can practically write your own paycheck. Trust me, once you start making that money," Anna rubbed her fingers together, putting an emphasis on money, "you will never want to be on someone's time clock."

"She's right. This job has helped me pay my way through med school." Jeff chimed in.

I was feeling excited until Destini walked in and interrupted our conversation.

"Oh, Chloe is not going to be an operator. She's going to be our new receptionist,"

"But I thought-"

Destini held up her hand. "I know what we discussed, but Lena just quit, so I'm going to need you to take her place for a while, at least until I find someone new."

"Okay," I said disappointedly; I was really looking forward to 'writing my own paycheck.'

"Come on. I'll show you around." She smiled.

We went into the small kitchenette. There was a door next to the refrigerator that led to a large basement. There were four small rooms, two on each side of the ample space. Each room had an inside window and its own private door. In the center of the floor was an oval-shaped desk, equipped with a desktop computer and a telephone.

"This is where it all happens," Destini said, stopping at the desk.

"Interesting," I said, as I took in the layout and décor of the space.

All the rooms, including the receptionist area, were painted soft red and had dim lighting. There was a computer on each desk along with a red telephone. On the wall in front of the oval desk was a forty-two-inch television and around the room were poster-sized erotic pictures hanging on the walls. Some of those positions on the images I never knew were possible.

"This will be your desk here," Destini said, bringing me out of my muse. "When the callers call in, you will ask them a few questions just to see which person would be best suitable for their needs. Here are the questions." She pointed to the index card taped to the desk by the phone. "This card is to stay here at all times."

I nodded, and she continued.

"On the phone, there are eight lines. The first four lines go to the four rooms down here." She pointed to each room, making sure to point out the numbers above each door. "Line one goes to room one, Line two goes to room two and so on." She explained. "Lines five through seven go to the three bedrooms upstairs. My line is five. Jeff's line is six, and seven was Lena's room, but now that she is leaving, it will be vacant."

"What about line eight?" I asked.

"Line eight goes to the den upstairs." "Okay, I got it. So, what's my schedule?"

"You will work from five in the evening until midnight Wednesday through Saturday. I know you have morning classes, so you are welcome to stay here in Lena's old room until we get a new roommate."

"And how much is the pay?"

"I will start you out with sixteen dollars and fifty cents an hour."

"You have a deal. It's way better than the twelve dollars an hour I make in the cafeteria." I chuckled.

Destini and I talked a little longer. By the time I left, I was feeling very excited about my new job.

Destini

I worked with Kendra Lee for two years at Fantasy. After she graduated, she married her college sweetheart and moved to New York. Her parents allowed Jeff and me to continue living in the house with an agreement to pay rent. As for Fantasy, well, she passed it on to me, and I was thrilled at the opportunity to have my own business. Jeff stayed on as an operator, and I hired Anna, Tyson, and Lena as additional phone operators. Lena couldn't handle some of the requests from the callers, so I made her a receptionist, which turned out to be a great thing because we didn't have to stay close to the phones all day. She would give the call to whoever fit the caller's request.

The business was great. Our call volume had increased, so I decided to hire another operator.

Anna had told me her friend Lacey was interested in the job. I called Lacey and scheduled to meet her at the university during her free time. However, after speaking with her, I didn't think she would be a good match for Fantasy. She was just too immature for my liking.

I went to the cafeteria to see what other potential candidates I could find. I found an empty table in the far corner of the room, which gave me a good view of everyone. It wasn't long before my eyes settled on Chloe.

She was a natural beauty. Her face was free of make-up, and her hair was pulled back in a ponytail neatly tucked under a cap. She worked with ease as she multi-tasked behind the counter.

I waited forty-five minutes before I was able to speak with Chloe, and I'm glad I did. Not only did she become an employee, but she also became my best friend.

Chloe was hired as our receptionist, but when things were slow, I would let her listen in on some of my calls. I remember the first call she listened to. There was no one downstairs but the two of us. We were chatting at her desk when the phone rang. She answered it and went through her list of questions before putting the caller on hold.

"Hey, this guy wants a golden shower experience. Do you want to take it?"

"Sure, tell him to hold on." I took the garbage bag out of the trash can.

"Hold on sugar, I'm going to transfer you to Candi's line," she said, placing him on hold again.

I grabbed two, one-liter bottles of water and a roll of paper towels from the supply closet. I put several sheets of paper towels at the bottom of the trash can and opened both bottles of water. I then put the telephone on the speaker. I looked at Chloe and put my index finger to my mouth.

"Shhhh," I said to her in a low whisper.

She nodded.

"Hello, babe," I said in a seductive voice. "This is Candi daddy, what can I help you with today?"

He cleared his throat. "I want a golden shower."

"Okay, big daddy, that will be eighty dollars."

"Alright."

"Are you paying debit or credit?"

"Credit."

Chloe entered his card information into the computer for approval. Once everything went through, I was ready to perform.

"Alright, babe, are you ready?"

"Yes."

"Tell me how you want it, nice and slow or fast."

"Nice and slow."

I put my index finger over the opening of the bottle of water. "Okay, here it comes, babe," I said as the water drained from the bottle, hitting the paper towel in the trash can.

"Do you like the way that feels on your chest, babe?" I asked.

"Mhmm." he moaned. "It's so hot."

"Oh yeah, babe, rub it all over your body," I instructed as the water kept flowing.

"Ah, pee on my face," he said. He was getting more into it now.

Chloe's eyes got wide, and she pretended like she was about to throw up. I shook my head and shrugged my shoulders.

"Oh, you dirty boy." I poured the water a little faster. How you like that, babe?"

He started to gurgle.

Chloe mouthed, "What the hell!"

He moaned louder. The more I poured, the louder he moaned, until he reached his climax. Afterward, he hung up without saying a word.

"Girl, what in the hell was that! I was afraid he was going to get strangled."

"Honey, that goes with the territory. You just have to do your part to get them there. Some clients will use their own props to make it seem more real to them, but I don't mind, just pay me my money," I said, rubbing my fingers together.

She gave me a high-five. "I heard that."

THE WEDDING

Destini

As I walked towards my future husband, I took in the ambiance of the room. The light refracting from the crystal chandeliers made everything look so elegant. It was like a picture out of a magazine.

At the left side of the altar stood my ten bridesmaids, all dressed in yellow, V-neck, chiffon dresses that came just above their knees. The groomsmen stood proudly at the right side of the altar in their gray tuxedos, with a yellow rose pinned to their jackets. The flower girls had left a trail of yellow and white roses down the aisle before taking their assigned positions beside the bridesmaids.

There were a lot of thoughts running through my head, like, am I really ready for marriage? Will he love me despite all my imperfections? And so on.

I'm not going to lie, I was nervous as hell, and by the way, Devin was wiping the sweat from his face. I knew he was nervous, too.

When I approached him, and he took my hand, my nerves settled a little until we exchanged our vows. I noticed when he said I love you, he was

looking at Chloe and not me. That was a stab in my heart. After all, we've gone through these past few months, I thought, we were getting closer. We will be having a baby soon, and I'm confident Chloe will be a thing of the past, as soon as our bundle of joy gets here. I just have to be patient.

Chloe

I observed Destini as she walked down the aisle on her wedding day. She looked stunning in her strapless, off-white, mermaid style wedding gown covered in sequins from top to bottom, which fit her perfectly.

Her hair was in an up-do with a waterfall of curls cascading down the middle of her back. She looked straight ahead with her eyes fixated on Devin; her soon to be husband, who stood patiently waiting for her at the altar.

He wiped beads of sweat from his forehead with the white handkerchief he pulled out of the pocket of his pants and quickly tucked it inside of his jacket. I could tell he was nervous, and he should've been. He was marrying the wrong woman, and he knew it. Hell, the way he made love to me, just before the ceremony proved it.

When the pastor told Devin that he could kiss his bride, I was smiling on the outside. But still, tickled pink on the inside, because the way he had dipped his tongue in my Reese's cup earlier, I knew she couldn't help but taste my sweetness.

During the reception, the bridal party sat with the bride and groom at the same table. I was the matron of honor, so I got to sit next to Devin, which worked out great when the lights were turned off for the dancing part of the evening.

While Destini was busy line dancing with family and friends on the dance floor, Devin was busy doing a little finger dancing of his own. Soft moans escaped my mouth as my body shivered with pleasure from the assault on my budding flower. He removed his fingers from inside of me and sucked them one at a time, savoring the essence of my nectar. Just as I unzipped his pants, the music stopped, and Destini walked over to the table. He picked up his glass and took a sip of wine. I followed his lead and did the same.

When she sat down, I stood to leave.

"I'm going to head on home and let you love birds have at it," I said, polishing off the last bit of wine in my glass.

"Aww, I'll walk you out." Destini stood.

"No. Stay. I'll be fine." I gave her a hug, then hugged Devin. "Good night, you two." I smiled and walked away.

On the way home, I cried. The truth is, my heart was broken. The thought of Devin not coming back with me tore me up inside. I thought about how Destini would get to sleep with him every night and wake up with him every morning. "Life just isn't fair!" I screamed.

When I arrived home, I opened the door and laid my purse and keys down on the small table in the foyer. I had barely settled in when my cell phone vibrated in my hand. It was a message from Devin. **I LOVE YOU. I'll see you soon.** As I stared at those three words, a tear rolled down my cheek. "I'm supposed to be your wife," I uttered.

I walked into the kitchen, grabbed a bottle of red wine from the wine rack on the counter, and headed to the bedroom to drink away my sorrow.

Devin

"I made a mistake."

"What you mean you made a mistake? Bruh, you are married now!" Ricky retorted.

"I know."

"So, what are you going to do?"

"I don't know. Apart of me wants to annul this marriage, but the other part of me is telling me to stay, for the sake of the baby."

"If you're not happy, what makes you think that's going to be good for the baby?"

"Man, I don't know."

"Where's Destini?"

"She's in the room."

"Well, if she's in the room, where are you?"

"Down at the bar."

"What! Devin, it's your wedding night."

"Don't you think I know that?" I said, annoyed.

"Man, I told you to hold off on getting married. Hell, who gets married in three months anyway. You've only known her for what, four, four and a half months?"

"Yeah, but her daddy was on her case about having a child out of wedlock."

"So what? She's not the first woman to ever have a child out of wedlock, and she won't be the last."

I sighed. "I know, Ricky. I was just trying to do the right thing. After all, it's my baby."

"Are you sure about that?"

"Well, she says it is mine."

"Just because she says it's yours doesn't make it so. Man, you know you can't trust a female these days. You should've waited and got a DNA test."

"Well, it's too late for all that now, isn't it? I snapped.

"Not really, but we can discuss that at another time," he said, ignoring my attitude.

"Yeah, that's probably best. Right now, I'm in a bad headspace."

"I can tell, but it's going to be alright."

"I sure hope so."

"Hey, you know I got your back, right?"

"Always, no doubt. Look bruh, I'll holler at you later."

"Okay, peace," Ricky said, hanging up the phone.

Ricky Lane is my boy. We grew up together. He has always had my back, and I have always had his. Ricky is a no non-sense kind of dude. He keeps it real no matter what, and that's what I love about him. He's always given me the truth, whether I liked it or not.

I finished my beer and went back to the room where I found Destini lying in bed watching television.

"Where have you been?" She asked with attitude.

"I was downstairs at the bar."

"Really, on our wedding night!" She threw her hands in the air to further express her disapproval.

"Destini, don't act like-" I stopped talking to avoid saying something I would regret later.

"Don't act like what?"

"Nothing, just drop it."

I grabbed my shower bag and left for the bathroom. When I returned to the bedroom, the television was off, and Destini had her back turned towards my side of the bed. I between the sheets and tried to touch her, but she pulled away. What a first night this has turned out to be. I rolled over with my back to hers.

Closing my eyes, I thought about Chloe. I could see her beautiful round bottom, bent over the sink in the small linen closet at the church. I liked the way she called my name when I entered her from behind. I could still feel her wetness moistening my rod as it slipped in and out of her. "Mmmm," I moaned.

"Wake the hell up!" Destini hit me in the back.

"Ouch! Woman, what the hell is wrong with you?" I quickly leaned over and turned on the bedside lamp.

"You are what's wrong with me! That must have really been one hell of a dream!"

"What are you talking about?"

"I'm talking about you over there with all that moaning and grinding, waking me out of my damn sleep!"

"Really, Destini, I have no control of that!" I rubbed the back of my shoulder, trying to soothe the pain. "You better not hit me like that again."

"Who was she?"

"Who was who?"

"Don't play dumb with me, Devin."

"Destini, it was just a dream."

She paused. "Just a dream, huh. Okay." She snatched the covers over her head and turned her back to me again. Why bother. I laid down and eventually fell asleep.

Chloe

I don't remember what time I fell asleep, but the familiar sound of my ringtone was my wakeup call.

"Good morning, sleepyhead."

"Good morning, Destini."

"I just wanted to let you know we were leaving for the airport."

"Ok, have fun, and be safe."

"We will," she chirped.

I could picture that big Kool-Aid smile on her face, and I hated it with every fiber of my being.

"Alright, call me when you get there and tell Devin I said hello," I said, trying to disguise the discontentment in my voice.

"I will. Well, we will see you in a week. I love you, sis."

I rolled my eyes. "I love you, too."

I know what you're thinking, but you're wrong. I do love Destini. I just have to find a way to forgive her.

Devin

The following morning, we ate breakfast in silence. The twenty-minute ride to the airport seemed like hours. Destini didn't say one word to me on the way there. If this was any indication of how the honeymoon was going to be, then it was going to be one hell of a week in Jamaica, and I meant that in the worst way.

Ironically, the plane ride was great. We were able to watch a movie on the plane, which was fine by me since Destini was still angry. I figured I would give her some space, and when we got settled in our room, I would try to smooth things out.

When the taxi driver turned into the driveway of The Oasis by The Sea resort, it looked like we had stepped into paradise. The grounds were manicured, and the flowers were at full bloom.

"Here we are," The driver said, getting out of the car and collecting our bags from the trunk. He placed them on the luggage carrier that the young bellhop had brought to the vehicle.

"Thank you," I said, and handed him a tip.

"Enjoy your stay." He smiled and tipped his hat before driving off.

Once we were in the room, I pulled Destini down onto my lap.

"Babe, let's talk," I said, rubbing the small of her back. She didn't protest, but she didn't speak either. "Destini, how long are you going to give me the silent treatment?" Still, she said nothing. "Look, we are on our honeymoon, for goodness sake. Let's talk about this so we can move on." I tried to reason.

"As soon as you tell me why you called out Chloe's name last night during all that moaning and groaning you were doing, we can move on."

"Destini, stop playing." I gave her that 'be for real' look.

She crossed her arms. "I'm not playing! I'm serious."

I held my hands up. "I was asleep. I don't even remember having a dream. You can't hold me responsible for something I said in my sleep."

She looked into my eyes as if she was trying to read my soul. "Alright, I'm going to let it go." She stood. "I think I'll go take a dip in the pool."

"Can I come along?"

"No, I would like to be alone. I need time to think."

"Destini, you are giving this more energy than it deserves."

"Maybe, but I'm still in my feelings right now."

"Okay, have it your way," I said, letting it go.

She pulled her bathing suit out of her suitcase and went into the bathroom to change. When she closed the door, I fell back on the bed. *Damn, I can't believe I slipped and called Chloe's name last night. I got to be more careful.* I thought as I covered my face with the pillow.

When Destini left for the pool, I decided to take a walk on the beach. I stopped by the bar and ordered a Jamaican *me crazy*. It was the specialty drink of the day suggested by the bartender. She was a gorgeous, black, voluptuous woman with beautiful brown eyes and a smile that could brighten any bad day. I knew I had to get out of there, and I had to get out quickly before I got myself in more trouble.

As I walked along the beach, I took in the atmosphere. The white-sand beaches and the clear blue water was breathtaking, almost enchanting. A feeling of sadness came over me, and I called Chloe.

"Hello," she answered on the second ring. "Hey, you," I said, happy to hear her voice.

"Devin, let me call you back."

"Okay." I managed to say before the line went dead.

I found a beach chair under an umbrella and sat down while I waited for Chloe to call me back.

Destini

When I got to the pool, I was happy to see the poolside bar open. I sat on a barstool and patiently waited to be served.

Carlos, the bartender, finally made his way over to me. First impression, He was cute. But compared to Devin, he didn't stand a chance. He was of average height, brown complexion, with hazel eyes, he was slender build, and had a gorgeous smile. Devin, on the other hand, is just the opposite. He's six foot four, dark complexion, and all muscles.

"Hello ma'am, what can I get you?" Carlos said, interrupting my thoughts.

"Let me have a frozen Pina Colada." "Coming right up." He smiled.

Funny, I didn't notice his dimples until then. I turned around and watched the people hanging out at the pool. Some were in the water, while others were either sunbathing, reading a book, or just talking and enjoying their drinks.

"Here, you are ma'am."

Carlos sat the drink down on the counter in front of me.

"Thank you." I handed him a ten-dollar bill and stood from my seat to leave. "Keep the change."

I spotted a vacant chair under a palm tree.

After getting comfortable, I called Chloe.

"Hello," she answered.

"Hey girl, what are you doing?"

"I'm working. What are you doing?

"Devin and I are not speaking."

"What do you mean you're not speaking?"

"Just what I said," I retorted.

"Destini, what happened?"

"He called out another woman's name in his sleep."

"What!"

"Yep, so I got mad."

"Okay, well, whose name did he call?"

"Lisa."

There was a brief pause, and I knew she was processing the words that I had spoken.

"Listen, Destini. You can't hold the man accountable for what he said in his sleep. That's just wrong."

"That's what he said."

"Well, he's right. This is your honeymoon. You should be enjoying each other, not walking around mad."

"Yeah, I thought about that, too." I sighed.

"Good. Now go find Devin and put it on him, honey."

We both laughed. "I guess you're right," I said, feeling much better.

"I know I'm right. Hold on."

A couple of minutes passed before Chloe returned to the phone.

"Hey, sorry about that. Are you okay now?" She asked.

"Yes. Thanks for listening."

"No problem, I'm always here for you."

"I know. I love you, Chloe."

"Love you, too."

"Bye."

"Bye."

As I sat there finishing my drink, I reevaluated my conversation with Chloe. I knew she was right. I needed to fix things with Devin, and the sooner, the better.

Had he called any other woman's name; I probably wouldn't have given it so much energy. But it was Chloe's name he called, and that had me in my feelings.

Chloe is a beautiful woman. She's five feet six, with honey-brown skin, and a perfect coke bottle shape. But, by comparison, I'm five feet five, and I'm also a honey-brown complexion. I'm not as curvy as she is, but I can still hold my own. I guess if you had to have a mental picture of us, we'd be like Beyoncé and Alicia Keys, her being Beyoncé and me, Alicia.

Devin

I felt my cell phone vibrate and pulled it out of my pocket. It was from Chloe.

"Hello."

"Hey, I'm sorry about that, I was on another call."

"No problem."

"So, what's going on?" She asked.

"You done got me in trouble," I said with a light chuckle.

"I've got you in trouble. How did I get you in trouble?"

"I called your name out last night while I was trying to rub one out."

"Tell me you didn't do that."

I could sense her amusement. "Shiddd, yes, I did, and now your girl is tripping. We're barely talking."

"Yeah, I know. I was on the phone with her when you called me, that's why I had to call you back."

"Oh, so it's like that?"

"What do you mean?"

"You were supposed to hang up with her and talk to your man."

"Correct me if I'm wrong, but didn't you marry her? So actually, you're her man, not mine."

"I see, it's like that, huh? I know what you need."

"What is it you think I need, Devin?"

"You need some get right," I said, matter-of-factly.

"Hmm, some get right, huh, Mr. Johnson?" She teased.

"That's right, and I'm going to give it to you when I get back, so be ready."

"Oh, I'll be ready, you just make sure you have enough energy for me, big boy."

"Don't you worry about that. It's going to be on."

"Okay, we'll see."

"Indeed, we will."

Putting all the joking aside, my mood became more serious. "Chloe, I miss you like crazy. I messed up big time."

"Yeah, you did."

I could hear the sadness in her voice, and it made my heartache. "It wasn't supposed to be like this. I wish I could go back to that night."

"Yeah, me, too," she sighed.

"Man, this whole situation is jacked up."

"Devin, let's change the subject. I don't want to talk about it."

I ignored her. I needed to talk about it. I wanted her to know how I truly felt.

"I never meant to hurt you, Chloe."

"I know. I can't put all the blame on you. I played a part in it. too."

"Yeah, but I let my guard down. I'm sorry, babe," I said, apologizing for what felt like the thousandth time.

"I'm sorry, too."

The pain I caused her was killing me. I hated what I had done to her, to us.

"I'll call you tomorrow, okay?"

"I'll be waiting," she said and ended the call.

I looked at my phone and saw that I had a message from Destini. **We need to talk**. I sighed heavily. Now was not the time to have a talk. I needed to clear my head.

Reflection

I thought about the day I met Chloe. We were at the GBM banquet, and she was standing outside of the women's restroom when I walked out of the men's bathroom.

"Hey, will you watch the door while I use the men's restroom? Whoever is in there is in no rush to come out," she said before she dashed into the men's restroom and closed the door behind her.

I stood and waited for her to come out, like the gentleman that I am.

"Thank you," she said, with much gratitude when she opened the door.

"You're welcome. Did you wash your hands?" I teased.

She placed one hand on her hip. "Oh, you have jokes. Of course, I washed my hands." We both laughed.

"Well, I say, I'm owed a dance later for keeping a watch out for you." I smiled.

"Is that right," she said, playing along.

"That's right."

She smiled. "Well, I think that could be arranged."

"May I walk you back to your table?"

I offered her my arm. "I'm Devin Johnson, by the way."

"Chloe Miller."

She interlocked her arm with mine, and we walked back to her table. I pulled her chair out. Once she was seated, I bent down and whispered in her ear.

"I'll be back for my dance."

She looked at me and smiled. Every now and then, I would glance her way, and our eyes would lock for a brief moment until our gaze was broken either by another guest or one of us looking away.

That night, I got my dance. In fact, I got quite a few dances and a date for the next weekend.

We had been in a great place. Our relationship was growing stronger each day, and I had fallen in love with her. I had even told my homeboys Ricky and A.J that I was going to marry Chloe, but that didn't happen, and I'm to blame for that. If I'd just gone to the bedroom with Chloe instead of staying behind to hang out with A.J., Sonya, and Destini, things would've turned out differently. But that night, I was down for any and everything.

Chloe had gone to the bedroom, and we were all sitting around the table laughing, talking, and throwing back shots of tequila. While smoking their joint, Sonya whispered in Destini's ear, and they started kissing.

A.J and I looked at each other and said in unison, "damn, it's like that!" Destini broke her kiss with Sonya and started kissing A.J., Then she began rotating between the two.

Afterward, Destini put her hand on my thigh. She started traveling towards destination hardwood, but I stopped her before she got there. She poked her bottom lip out like a pouting child and stood from the table and took her shirt off; then, she removed her bra. She pinched her nipples, then put one of them in A.J.'s mouth. Sonya quickly took the other one in her mouth without hesitation. Destini threw her head back, making sounds of pleasure. I ain't gone lie. I was harder than a brick. Destini pushed both of their heads back and walked over to the couch. With the crook of her finger, she beckoned them to join her.

They sat on the sofa while Destini stood in front of them. Seductively, she pulled down her shorts and stepped out of them, running her fingers through the band of her black, lace G-string, then turned her back to us. She bent over in front of A.J., and he kissed her butt cheeks. While pulling down her G-string. Sonya, on the other hand, was getting undressed. A.J. pulled Destini onto his lap and palmed both of her breasts, caressing her nipples while placing kisses on the back of her neck.

Sonya got on her knees in front of Destini and put her face right in the pudding. Destini started out with low moans, but the more Sonya licked, the louder she got until she climaxed.

That's when Chloe came into the living room. After she got over the shock of what was taking place, I convinced her that we should join the party and we took it to her bedroom.

Sonya and Destini undressed Chloe right away. While Sonya showed Chloe extra attention, Destini turned hers to me. First, she teased the tip of my head, rotating her tongue around my rod until she had all my inches down her throat. That shit was impressive. I've never had a girl to do that before, not even Chloe.

Destini had my head spinning, and all common sense went out the window. Just as I was about to explode, she stopped, sat on the wood, and rode me to destination ejaculation. I was done, and I mean that literally. Because Destini got pregnant that night, and I lost the woman I love, along with the future I wanted.

Destini

When I got back to the room, Devin was sitting up in the bed, with a beer in his hand, watching television.

"Can we talk? I asked, joining him on the bed.

He took a swallow of his beer. "Not now."

I snatched the remote out of his hand and turned the television off. "Now is a perfect time."

He looked at me but didn't say anything. I could tell he was pissed by the way his muscle twitched in his jaw.

"Devin, I really want us to work this out."

"I thought we already did." He grabbed the remote out of my hand and turned the television back on.

"Okay, have it your way." *I know what you need,* I thought, as I got comfortable on the bed and unzipped his pants.

"What are you doing?"

"I'm getting ready to blow your mind."

Devin pulled me into his arms. "Whew, that was good?" He grinned.

"My pleasure." I winked and laid my head on his chest.

"Destini, I'm sorry for how I made you feel. I didn't try to hurt you; it was just a dream."

"I know, and I'm sorry for making such a big deal out of it. I know you had no control over that."

I kissed him on the mouth. We talked a little longer, before settling down to take a nap.

I stretched my arms above my head. "What time is it?"

Devin looked at his watch. "It's seven o'clock."

"Seven o'clock," I repeated.

Our little nap had lasted longer than we intended.

"Yes, let's get up from here and go get some dinner," he said, getting out of the bed.

"I'm down with that."

We ate dinner at The Pelican Grill, which was reco-mmended by our taxi driver. It turned out to be a great choice. The food was delicious, and the ambiance of the place was charming.

We had a great conversation. We talked about the baby, our future, and the things we both wanted to accomplish individually, and together. We were back on track, and I, for one, was happy about that.

After dinner, we retreated to our room for a nightcap of passionate lovemaking.

The following morning, I woke up before Devin, so I decided to take a shower. As the warm water hit my skin, I thought about Chloe, and the advice she had given me. I smiled. I will definitely have to do something special for her when we return home.

Part Two:
What's Done in The Dark

Destini

I took an additional week off from work to unpack and organize our new home. As I placed a box on the table labeled Devin, my cell phone rang.

"Hello," I said, thankful for the break. "Hello, Ms. Rivera, this is Olivia from the post office. I was calling to let you know your package has come in."

"Thank you, Olivia, I will be there shortly," I said, before hanging up the phone.

I stopped what I was doing, grabbed my keys and purse off the nightstand, and headed to the post office.

When I walked into the building, I saw Belinda - Ricky's wife, standing in line. There were two other people behind her, which was great for me because I really did not care to be social with her. She is very nosey and is always trying to get into our business. I really need to talk to Devin about it because he has been telling Ricky way too much of it lately.

We had dinner at their house after we returned from our honeymoon, and he told them about the dream incident. I'm glad he didn't reveal that it was Chloe's name he'd called out. However, that didn't stop Ms. Nosey from asking questions.

Ricky finally told her to let it go before she stopped asking for details. I was glad he intervened. I didn't want to ruin our evening, but I was two seconds from cursing her ass out.

"Hey girl, how are you?" she said, noticing me as she scanned the back of the line.

"I'm fine, and you?"

"I'm great." She let the two customers behind her, move ahead of her.

Oh, God, help me. I plastered a fake smile on my face. "Are you working today?" I asked, trying to be cordial.

"Yes, I just came by to mail off this box of hair back to the distributor. They sent me the wrong brand."

Belinda is a great hairstylist. I'll give her that, but she's just too messy. In the short time, I've gotten to know her, I've learned, she can't hold water, and she's an instigator, always throwing stones and hiding her hands behind her back.

"Girl, you should stop by, so I can touch up those edges," she smirked.

This Heifer is trying to throw shade. "Maybe some other time. I have an appointment with my hairstylist this weekend."

"Mmhmm. Well, I must say you are looking mighty small to be four months pregnant. Honey, when I was four months pregnant, I couldn't fit in my regular clothes, I had to go out and buy new ones, because of my baby bump.

"Yeah, you mentioned that when we were at your house for dinner," I said sarcastically.

"Next," the clerk announced. It was really just to get Belinda's attention. She was so busy looking me over, she wasn't paying attention to the line.

After she finished handling her business, she turned and looked at me.

"See you later, girl." She waved goodbye. "You have a great day," I said, relieved, she didn't hang around.

I walked up to the counter. "I'm here to pick up a package."

"What's your name?"

"Destini Rivera."

"I need to see your ID."

I handed the clerk my driver's license. She looked it over and gave it back to me.

"One moment," she said and left in search of my package.

Shortly after, she returned with a box in her hand. I signed the form, verifying I received the package and left.

I stopped by Moms 2 Be and picked up a couple of maternity shirts before heading home. When I pulled in the driveway, Chloe pulled in behind me. Aww, hell, really. I took a deep breath and got out of the car.

"Hey love, how are you?" Chloe asked.

"Not too well. I'm just getting home from the doctor and was about to go in and lay down."

"Oh, well, I'm not going to bother you. I had spoken with Devin earlier, and he told me you were unpacking, so I came by to offer you a hand."

"I was unpacking, but I started cramping, so I went to the doctor."

"Is everything alright?"

"Yeah, we are both doing fine."

"Can I do anything?"

"No, I just need to get some rest." I smiled, hoping she would get the hint and leave.

"Okay, call me if you need me."

"I will."

She hugged me. "Love you."

"I love you, too."

Chloe got in her car but didn't back out the driveway until I was in the house. I stood and watched her through the living room window. After she had driven off, I went out to the car and grabbed the box and the bag of maternity shirts and hurried back into the house.

I got a knife from the kitchen drawer to cut the tape on the package. Inside the box were my twenty-week, twenty-eight-week, and thirty-eight-week fake baby bumps.

I read the directions and tried each bump on with my new maternity shirts. Everything fit perfectly. I took the twenty-eight-week and thirty-eight-week bellies and locked them in the chest box I had in my closet. All that was left was to figure out my next plan of action.

Chloe

When I left Destini, I immediately called Devin.

"Hi, I just left your house, and Destini says she's not feeling well."

"Did she say what was wrong?"

"Yeah, she said she was cramping. She went to the doctor. Everything is fine, and she's going to go to bed."

"Okay. I'll give her a call later," he sighed.

"Are we still on for two o'clock?"

"Well, I guess that will depend-"

"That will depend on what?" He interrupted.

"On whether or not you will be going home to take care of Destini."

"Don't worry about that. I will be there at two."

"Okay, then, I will see you there, Mr. Johnson."

"See you soon."

I looked at the clock on the car dashboard. It was twelve-thirty. I headed home to grab a couple of things before I met up with Devin.

As soon as I closed the front door behind me, the house phone ranged.

"Hello."

"Hello, Chloe, you've been hard to catch up with."

"Who is this?"

"Don't worry. You will find out soon enough."

"What do you want?"

He gave a wicked laugh and took a deep breath.

"You know, you looking thick in those jeans."

"I don't know who you are, but if you call, here again, I am going to call the police." I slammed the phone on the receiver. I looked out the window. There was nothing out of the ordinary. I turned around, and Anna was standing there with a frightened look on her face.

"Chloe, are you alright?"

Without waiting for me to answer, she went on to explain that she had picked up the phone at the same time I did but didn't say anything when she heard me speak.

"What do you think about that call?" I asked, a little shaken, but trying to keep it together.

She picked up the phone and handed it to me. "I think you should call the police."

"You're probably right, but it could just be a prank. If he calls back again, I will call the police."

She nodded. "Well, you be careful."

"I will, I promise." I gave her a hug and hurried upstairs to pack a small bag.

I was putting my bag in the trunk of the car when I observed an older gentleman looking through the windows of the abandoned house across the street.

"Excuse me," he yelled to get my attention as he crossed the street. "Can you tell me who owns that property?" He pointed back at the house.

"I'm not sure who owns it, but there's a sign-" *hmm, what happened to the sign?* "Well, there was a sign right there this morning," I said, pointing at the area where the sign stood. "I think it's Limit Realtors. You will need to contact them.

"Okay, thanks, I'll give them a call," he said, before crossing the street, getting into his black Camaro and driving away.

"I received the strangest call today." I propped up on my elbow and faced Devin.

"How so?"

"This guy said he's had a hard time catching up with me, but when I asked him what he wanted, he said, and I quote, "you know, you looking thick in those jeans." Devin raised an eyebrow.

"I asked him for his name, and his response was, "you'll soon find out."

"Hmm, did you, by any chance, recognize his voice?"

"No."

"Have you had an encounter with anyone lately?"

"No. Well yes, today there was this guy across the street looking at the vacant house. He asked me did I know who owned it."

"What did he look like?"

"He was tall, light complexion, medium build, and well dressed. Oh, and he had dreadlocks about neck length."

Devin nodded. "I see you really paid attention to him," he said sarcastically.

"First of all, he was standing right in front of me."

"Yeah, well, did you notice anything strange about him? Did his voice sound like the guy on the phone?"

"No, he didn't seem strange at all. I mean, once I told him that he needed to get in touch with Limit Realtors, he said thank you and walked back to his car."

"What kind of car?"

"It was a black Camaro. Do you think it could have been him?"

"I can't really say, but it's probably not him. You be careful, and if he calls you again, try to ask him more questions, don't be so quick to hang up."

"Yes, sir, Officer Devin, sir," I smirked.

He flipped me onto my back and pinned both of my arms above my head with one hand while he tickled me with the other.

"I have told you about your mouth."

"Okay, okay," I yelled as I tried to squirm my way out of his grip. He let me go and kissed me on the mouth.

"Girl, you drive me crazy."

He spread my legs apart and kissed me deeply. I could feel his hardness throb between my thighs. I wrapped my legs around his waist, and he entered me. This time was different. It was like he was given me all of him, heart, mind, and soul.

Devin

When I arrived home, Destini was standing at the end of the driveway, talking to Mrs. Spinner, our neighbor.

"Hello, ladies, how are you doing?" I said, giving Destini a kiss on the cheek.

"We're fine." They both said in unison. "Honey, Mr. Spinner is in the hospital."

"I'm sorry to hear that."

"Thank you. He suffered a heart attack yesterday, and I'm just here long enough to get some clothes, then I'm going back to the hospital."

"Is there anything we can do?" I asked.

"If, you two don't mind, keep an eye on the house for us and get our mail, please."

"Sure, no problem," Destini said, taking hold of Mrs. Spinner's hand.

"Well, I better get on in here and get my bag packed. Thank you again," she said before leaving.

"Your home pretty late tonight," Destini said as we walked into the house.

"Yeah, Pete had us stay over to look at a new case."

"Hold on." She held up a finger. "I have to go pee." She made a dash for the bathroom. "Your dinner is in the microwave," she yelled.

I put my things down and walked into the kitchen to heat my food. Destini had prepared beef tips in gravy, rice, cabbage, and cornbread. While my meal was heating, she came out of the bathroom.

"So, how are you feeling?" I asked.

"I feel much better, but I have some bad news."

"What is it?" My heart dropped, not knowing what to expect.

"I'm having some light bleeding, so the doctor said no more sex."

Relieved, I took a deep breath. "I thought you were going to tell me there was something wrong with the baby. No sex, that's cool, there are other inventive ways we can make it happen." I winked.

"Ooh, you are a dirty little man," she laughed.

"Hey, it's not dirty when you're married."

We continued to talk while I finished my dinner. Just when I finished eating, my cell phone rang.

"What's up?" I answered.

"Is now a good time."

"No."

"It's all set. I will sign the papers tomorrow."

"Great. Call me when it's done." I said, hanging up the phone.

"What was that about?" Destini asked. "The new case we are working on, and you know I can't discuss it so, don't ask."

"I know." She sighed. "The secret life of a cop."

"You got it."

I stood up from the table and kissed her on the forehead. "I'm going to take a shower."

Chloe

All day, I kept playing over and over in my head the strange call I received yesterday and found it hard to focus.

"Okay class, I will see you tomorrow. Have a good day," Mr. Dents announced.

The noise of the students preparing to leave interrupted my thoughts.

"Chloe, I would like to speak to you," he said, taking a seat at his desk.

When everyone left, I approached his desk.

"Chloe, you were not very attentive today, is everything alright?"

"I'm sorry, Mr. Dents. I just have a lot on my mind, that's all."

"I can tell. Is it anything I can help you with?"

"I'm not sure if anyone can help me with this."

He leaned back in his chair. "Well, let's give it a try. What's the problem?"

I could tell he was genuinely concerned. I trusted Mr. Dents, so I didn't have a problem telling him what was going on.

"I received a phone call yesterday from a strange man, and I'm trying to make sense of it all."

He leaned forward. "What did he say?"

"He said that I've been hard to catch up with and when I asked him what he wanted, he said, I looked thick in my jeans, and I will find out soon enough who he was."

"Hmm, I see." He stroked his chin. "Did you call the police?"

"Well, not officially, but you know my boyfriend is a cop, and I told him about it."

"Yeah, but you still need to make a report."

"I will if he contacts me again. It could've just been a prank." I shrugged.

"Chloe, don't take this lightly; call the police."

"I will."

"No. Call them now, so I can make sure it's done," he said firmly.

I put down my books, pulled my cell phone out of my purse, and made the call. When the officer arrived, I told him everything about the call. He asked if I had caller ID. I told him, yes, but I had failed to look at it. I told him I would check when I got home and give him a call.

When I got to my car, Sonya was waiting for me.

"Hey, what's going on? I saw you talking to the police when I passed by Mr. Dent's class."

"I was filing a report about a strange call I received yesterday from some guy."

"Do you think it could be the guy that's been calling you?"

"I hadn't thought about that. Is he still calling the apartment?"

"No, but a guy called about three or four days ago, from Excelle Bank, saying he   needed to talk to you about some fraudulent activity on your account."

"I don't bank at Excelle Bank. Is that even a bank?" I wondered.

"I don't know, Chloe. I told him you didn't live there and gave him your house number." She paused. "Oh my God, Chloe, I am so sorry, it didn't cross my mind that it could be that guy. He sounded so professional. I thought he was legit."

"That's okay. Do me a favor, when you get home, I need you to check your caller ID and see if you can find his phone number."

"Chloe, I deleted all of those numbers last night. Karen was complaining about the voicemail being full because no one could leave messages, so I deleted everything, the caller ID and voice mail."

"Damn," I said, not hiding my disappointment. Sonya, if he calls back, let me know."

"Okay, I will."

"Listen, I have to get home. I will talk to you later."

We hugged and went our separate ways.

On my way home, I kept looking in my rear-view mirror. I noticed a yellow canary jeep behind me, following a little too close for my comfort.

When I got to my neighborhood, I stopped at B's Convenient Store to be on the safe side. The jeep continued going. I waited ten minutes to see if the car would return before continuing home.

When I turned onto my street, the jeep was parked in front of the house across the street. A white female was standing on the lawn with the guy from yesterday. I took a deep breath. *Get it together, Chloe.*

As soon as I put the key in the front door to unlock it, the door flung open, and I lost my balance. Jeff quickly sprang into action and caught me before I fell.

"Whoa, I'm sorry, are you okay?"

"Yes, I'm fine. Where are you rushing off to?"

"I have a hot date tonight, and I'm going to get a fresh cut." He winked at me and smiled.

Jeff was not black, but he sure had a black swagger about him. I had to admit it was kind of sexy.

"Cool," I said, placing my books on the table in the foyer.

"Got to go, see you later."

I locked the door behind him and went to the basement. It was my shift, and I needed to relieve Anna.

When I opened the door, she was watching television.

"Hey, how have things been today?" I asked.

"Very slow." She turned down the volume on the TV. "Are you ready to take over the phones?"

"Not quite, just let me grab a quick snack, get my books, and I will be ready to go." She nodded and continued watching her show until I returned.

When Anna left, I settled in and turned off the television so I could study for an upcoming test in my chemistry class. About thirty minutes into my studying, the phone rang. I did my usual spill; then, things went left.

"Hold on, let me get Saucy for you." Saucy is a.k.a. Anna.

"Wait, hold on, sweet thing, I think I'd rather talk to you if that's alright."

Now, it wasn't what he said, but it was how he said it that made every hair on my neck stand up.

"I'll pay double what you charge." He offered, sensing my hesitation.

My mind was screaming no, but I didn't listen; after all, he just wanted to be spanked. I reasoned.

"Okay," I said, clearing my throat."

"Great, I have one request."

"What's that?"

"I want to reverse roles."

"Sure, I'll follow your lead, but that will cost you two- hundred dollars."

"No problem, I'm more than willing to pay for what I want."

Okay, big baller. After the transaction was complete, we began the role play.

"Picture yourself naked," he said in a light whisper.

"Mmm, I'm naked, babe," I said seductively.

"You're lying across my bed on your stomach."

"Ooh yeah, I can't wait." I purred.

"I don't want you to move, so I'm going to handcuff you to the bed rail."

"Mmhmm."

I was curious to see where he was going with this. I mean handcuffs, role reversal, really had me wondering what was up with this guy.

"I'm stroking you up and down your spine with a feather."

I released a light chuckle. "Ooh, that tickles."

"I grab an ice cube and rub it down your back, planting small kisses along the trail of the melted ice."

"Aww, that feels good."

"Yeah, you're starting to squirm, so I handcuff your legs to the bed rail, too."

"Then what, babe?"

"Now, I'm going to spank you."

Smack, it sounded like a light tap.

"Ooh, harder babe," I purred.

Smack! This time it sounded a little harder. "Ooh, you're getting me hot." I moaned.

"You like that baby girl?"

"Smack!"

"Oh, yes, babe."

"Let's see if you like this." His voice turned cold. "Chloe, you're going to die."

"Wha-what?"

I could not believe what I had just heard. There was nothing but pure evil in his voice.

"You heard me, Chloe. You're going to die. I'm going to gut you open like a fish," he spattered.

I quickly hung up the phone. It rang again, but I didn't answer it. I sat there, paralyzed and afraid.

Shortly after, Anna opened the door, and I jumped.

"Are you okay?" She asked.

"No, not at all, that psycho just called."

"Yeah, I know. That's why I came down here to tell you that he said he's coming for you."

I picked up the phone and called Officer Tanner.

"Hello."

"Officer Tanner, please."

"Speaking."

I completely fell apart. It was as if all the emotions of fear came pouring down on me at once.

"Officer Tanner, this is Chloe Miller, I talked to you earlier today at the university." I managed to say between sobs. "That guy just called me, and he threatened to kill me." I was now a complete basket case.

"Calm down, ma'am." I heard him say before Anna took the phone from out of my hand.

"Officer, Hi, I'm Anna, Chloe's roommate. She is very hysterical, but that guy told me to tell Chloe that he was coming for her, and I'm afraid of what he might do."

"That's understandable. What is your address?"

"123 Leonix Way."

"I'm on my way."

Ten minutes later, he was pulling in the driveway, and Devin pulled up right behind him.

"Ms. Miller, were you able to get a telephone number?" Officer Tanner asked.

"No. the number came up private."

"Are your calls recorded?"

"No."

"Yes," Devin interjected.

"What do you mean, yes?" I responded.

"Great, can you get me a copy of that call, ASAP," Officer Tanner interrupted. He looked back and forth between Devin and me. "Well, I'll be on my way. It's obvious you two need to talk."

"Yes, we do," I said, not taking my eyes off Devin.

"I'll get that recording to you, Tanner," Devin said, his eyes not wavering from mine.

Anna came up from the call center just in time to see Officer Tanner out to his car. When the door closed behind them, Devin started talking.

"Okay, before you get mad, let me explain." He placed his hand on my shoulders. I brushed his hand off and walked over to the couch to sit down.

"How long have the calls been recorded?"

He sat down next to me. "Since Destini and I came back from our honeymoon."

"What!"

"Sonya told Destini about the phone calls you had been receiving. When Destini told me about it, I told her it would be best if we had the calls recorded in case there was something up with this guy."

"So, you two didn't think I should know about this?"

"No. We wanted you to continue as normal, so the guy wouldn't get spooked."

"Is there anything else I need to know?"

"Yes, we also installed cameras around the house inside and outside with the exceptions of the bedrooms and bathrooms."

"OMG! How could you not tell me? Did Anna and Jeff know about this?"

"No, and don't tell them. Not yet, anyway."

"They have a right to know."

"You're right, they do, but not right now. The less they know, the better, trust me."

Then it occurred to me. All the times, Devin would stop by just to get a quickie or our explicit telephone conversations all recorded. I looked at him with panic on my face.

"Don't worry, it's all deleted. I have control of it from my phone. I'm not a rookie at this surveillance thing." He winked. He stood and took my hand in his. "Come, walk me to the door," he said, leading the way. He gave me a quick hug and left.

Destini

"Chloe, it was for your protection. You are my sister, and I love you. I'd do it again if I had to."

Chloe called me about the telephone call she received earlier. She also expressed her disapproval of me not informing her about the cameras and phone lines being recorded. I wanted to tell her, but Devin thought it was best she didn't know.

"Okay. Okay, Chloe, I will stop by Fantasy later, and we will finish this conversation. Right now, I have to get out of here and go pay bills." I lied, well sort of lied. I did have to leave but for an issue a little more personal than paying bills. However, I didn't feel like being interrogated, so I kept quiet.

I ended my call with Chloe and headed to the theater. I love old classic movies and had planned to catch a midday movie at Ole Skool Theater. The Five Heartbeats were showing, and it just so happened to be one of my favorite movies. I ordered my popcorn and coke and entered the theater room. I found the perfect seat and settled down for the film. I was in there by myself until an older couple came in just before the picture started.

During the film, the couple would sing along with the songs, and I found myself joining in with them. It was great; one of the best times I've had at a movie.

Walking back to my car, I was looking in my purse for my keys, when I was suddenly stopped.

"Oh, excuse me," I said, looking up at the tall gentlemen I had bumped into. I recognized him from the tire shop, but the lady standing beside him, I didn't know. I looked back and forth between the two of them.

"Hi, how are you doing?"

"I'm fine, and you?"

"I'm good."

"What movie did you see?" He asked.

"I watched The Five Heartbeats. It was great." I gave a thumbs up.

"That's what we are going to see. It's one of my favorite movies," she smiled.

"Yeah, well, she dragged me here. I just want to get through this so I can get home and watch the basketball championship game."

She hit him on his arm playfully, and we all laughed.

"I understand, my husband loves to watch the games, too."

"Oh, who is he rooting for?" He asked. "He likes the 69ers, but I think the Tigers are going to win this year."

"I like the 69ers, too. They are two and two with three games left, so it's not over until it's over."

"You're right, well you two enjoy the movie, I sure did." He nodded his head, and they went on their way.

I stopped by Fantasy for a few minutes just as I had promised Chloe. She was not there, but I did get a chance to see Anna and Jeff. Anna told me about the phone call Chloe received earlier that day, while Jeff sat and listened attentively.

"Destini, I'm really worried. I mean not only for Chloe's safety but ours," she said with a concerned look on her face.

"I know, but everything is going to be alright. We have officers patrolling the area throughout the day, and we have cameras inside and outside of the house." Jeff and Anna were both taken aback.

"Cameras!" They said in unison.

"Yes, cameras. They are everywhere except your bedrooms and the bathrooms."

"How long have we had cameras?" Anna asked.

"Since I came back from my honeymoon." Not giving them a chance to speak, I continued. "Chloe has been receiving these phone calls for a long time now, but they have never been as serious as the last couple of times he called."

"So, what's the game plan? Why hasn't this guy been caught?" Jeff asked.

"According to the detective, he has never approached the house. So, we don't know who or what we are dealing with?"

"You're dealing with a psychopath if you ask me," Anna said.

"Yeah, I agree." Jeff chimed in.

I nodded, "Well, I won't dispute that. I think you may be right, but just know we are trying our best to catch him." I stood to leave. "Tell Chloe I came by, and I will call her later."

Anna walked me out to my car.

"Uh, Destini, about those cameras." "Nothing to worry about. We only review them if necessary. Mainly when we've heard that Chloe received a call." I lied. I knew all about Anna's little shenanigans, but now was not the time to address them.

Chloe

Two weeks had passed, and I hadn't received any strange calls. I had finally begun sleeping at night, and things were getting back to normal.

"I talked to Ricky this morning, and he has me thinking," Devin said as we laid in bed, trying to catch our breath.

"About what?"

"About the baby."

I didn't say anything. I just listened as he continued.

"He and Belinda seem to think Destini is lying about the baby."

I sat up and looked at him. "What do you think?"

He ran his hand over his head. "I don't know what to think."

"Well, what about the pregnancy test?"

"I didn't see a pregnancy test."

"Okay, but you did go to the doctor with her, right?"

"Nope, she would always tell me about the doctor visit after she had gone."

"Devin, do you at least know who her doctor is? I mean, please tell me she has at least shown you some proof she is pregnant?" I asked, in disbelief.

He shook his head. "Nope, nada."

"So, you mean to tell me, you just took her word for it and married her!" I looked at him, dumbfounded.

"I know it sounds crazy."

"You damn right it sounds crazy!"

Now, I was mad as hell. All the changes we've had to endure, and he didn't even have proof that she was pregnant. My emotions were all over the place. I got out of bed and started getting dressed.

"Chloe, I was just trying to do the right thing."

"By marrying her! Did you consider me, us?"

"I did, babe, but I saw no way out."

He pulled me into his arms, and I began to sob. I was hurt. I mean, really hurt. It was as if I was reliving the day I first found out Destini was pregnant all over again. "I'm so sorry, Chloe." Devin kept repeating until I stopped crying. I wiped the tears from my eyes and stepped out of his embrace.

"Okay, this is what you're going to do. You are going to go to Destini's next doctor's appointment."

"Just how am I going to do that, when I don't know when her next appointment is?" He shook his head.

I threw my hands up and sat down on the bed.

"I'll talk to her and see if I can get some information out of her. In the meantime, you keep your eyes and ears open, okay."

"Alright." He wrapped his arm around my waist. "You know I love you, right."

"Yeah, I know. I love you, too."

Destini

"Hello," I said, struggling to keep the telephone to my ear. I had just put lotion on my hands, and they were slippery.

"What's up, big cousin!" The voice on the line squealed with excitement. I knew right away who it was.

"Ah snap, what is going on, my favorite cousin?" I said, sharing her excitement.

It had been a few months since I heard from Autumn, and I was so happy to hear from her.

We had practically grown up as sisters. After Autumn's dad died in the military, our Aunt Hattie, my father's sister, took her in and raised her as her own.

Autumn would stay with us when auntie had to work. That was until my dad received the opportunity to be a Criminal Law Judge and moved us out to California.

However, Autumn still spent every summer with us until she started college.

"Girl, I will be flying out to LA next month, and I thought maybe we could get together and hang out."

"Sure, that sounds great. How long are you going to be here?"

"A month. I have to get internship credits for one of my classes, and CSU accepted me. It's really only three weeks, but I figured I could spend a week just relaxing and hanging out with my favorite cousin."

"Awesome. So, where will you be staying?" I asked out of curiosity. *Here it comes.*

"I was hoping I could stay with you and Devin."

And there it goes. "Of course, cousin, you know you are always welcome," I said, with a smile to mask my true feelings.

I didn't mind her staying with me, but I didn't need her staying with me. Four weeks was a long time to try and keep my fake pregnancy from Autumn. She knows me better than anyone and would see right through my charades. I can't take that chance.

Suddenly, as if there was a light bulb in my head, I had the greatest idea.

"Autumn, you know what, it just crossed my mind. How would you like to stay in my bedroom at Fantasy? It will give you some space, and since Devin and I are new-."

"Say no more. I would be more than happy to stay at Fantasy so you two can have your privacy. I may even learn a thing or two while I'm there." she chuckled.

"Thanks, Autumn, for understanding."

"No problem, I will see you soon."

"Alright. See you soon. I Love you."

"I Love you, too," she said, ending the call.

Well, that's just great, as if things weren't as difficult already. I thought as I made a quick phone call.

"Hello."

"Hey, it's me, change of plans."

"What is it?"

"I need things to happen sooner. I don't have much time."

"How do you suppose we do that?

She's not due for another three months."

"I know that! I snapped. Find someone who is due like now! I have to have a baby within the next three weeks.

"You cannot have a full-term baby when you are only six months pregnant. It doesn't work that way," she said sarcastically.

"Now you listen to me. I am paying you a lot of money. I don't care what you have to do; just get me the damn baby."

"I'll see what I can do." She hung up the phone.

I started to call her back, but Devin pulled up in the driveway. I took a quick glance in the mirror and plastered a smile before opening the door as he walked up the steps.

"Hey, babe," I smiled.

"Hey, how's my favorite girl."

He wrapped his arms around my waist, giving me a light peck on the lips.

Liar. "I'm doing wonderful. Your dinner is in the microwave."

"Okay," he smiled and continued to the bedroom.

"So, how was your day?" I asked.

"Oh, it was fine. Same ole same ole."

He started to undress. I stood in the doorway as he removed each article of clothing. "I think I'll take a shower first before I eat my dinner. You want to join me?" He grinned.

I bent down to pick up his clothes. "No, you go ahead. I'm going to put in a load of clothes."

"Okay, be out in a few." He winked and walked into the bathroom.

Lawd all that chocolate, and I can't have any. I shook my head and walked out of the bedroom.

While Devin was in the shower, I took the opportunity to make another important phone call.

"Speak."

"We are going to have to push things up."

"When?"

"I need it to happen within the next couple of weeks."

"I'll get back to you."

"This is becoming a damn nightmare," I said to no one in particular.

"What's a nightmare?" Devin asked, standing behind me.

I clenched my chest. "Ooh, you scared me. I was just on the phone with customer service about the baby's crib that I ordered from Moms 2 Be. They called and said they didn't think they were going to be able to get that particular style crib. But we got it handled. Man, that was a quick shower," I said, trying to change the subject.

"I'm not done. I left my Bluetooth in my pants. Have you put them in the washer yet?"

"No, they're right here."

I pulled them out of the basket and handed them to him. He retrieved the Bluetooth and went to finish his shower. Meanwhile, I went into the living room to think. I was wondering just how much of my conversation Devin heard.

<h1 style="text-align:center">Devin</h1>

"Man, everything has been quiet. I mean nothing. It's as if this dude just disappeared," Officer Woods said.

"Hmmm, that is strange."

"Yeah, I know, but I can tell you that little Asian chick has been having a lot of visitors lately."

"Who, Anna?" I asked surprisingly.

Anna was usually to herself, or at least she was when I was around anyway.

"Yeah, she's up to something, but I don't think it has anything to do with Chloe. I mean, guys pick her up, and a few hours later, they drop her back off."

I raised an eyebrow. "You don't think Anna's doing what I think she's doing, do you?

"Now, you know, we've been in this business for a long time. If it walks like a duck and quacks like a duck, it's a duck."

I chimed in on the 'it's a duck' part.

"Hmm, well, keep your eyes open and keep me posted," I said, getting ready to leave.

"I will." We bumped fists, and I left.

When I got in my car, I called Chloe.

"Hey, what are you doing?" I asked.

"Eating a sandwich, what are you doing?"

"Coming to see you."

"I thought you were working today."

"I am, but I want to see you."

"Um, hmm, and why do you want to see me?" Her voice became sensual.

"You already know. I'm coming for that pudding and not the kind in a box, you down?"

"See you when you get here."

Five minutes later, I pulled up in the driveway. Before I could knock on the door, Chloe opened it and pulled me inside. She kissed me and led me upstairs to her bedroom.

"Where is everyone at?" I asked as we climbed the stairs."

"Jeff and Anna are in class right now."

"Well, who's working the phones?"

"I am. I had the lines transferred to my phone."

"Is that wise?" I stood in the doorway of her bedroom. She grabbed me by my belt and pulled me to her.

"Not on my cell phone, but my red phone," she said, pointing to the phone on her bedside table.

I nodded. A feeling of relief came over me. Although, I knew what Chloe did, even Destini, for that matter. I didn't want to hear the details of the operation mainly because I didn't like it, but that was their choice. However, now that Destini and I were married, I told her I didn't want her working at Fantasy anymore.

Chloe wrapped her arms around my neck, and we shared a passionate kiss.

"How long do we have?" She asked.

"This will have to be a quickie, babe. You know I can't be off the grid too long."

"Well, we better get started." She grinned.

Chloe

fter class, I headed to my car. There was a piece of paper nicely folded and tucked under my windshield wiper. I didn't think much of this because students are always leaving flyers on cars for some event or another.

When I unfolded the paper, I was petrified. It was a picture of Devin and I making love except my throat was cut, and blood was dripping down to the floor. The words **SOON, BABE** was written in the blood. My heart was pounding. I quickly got in my car and called Devin. I was thankful for Google's hands-free dialing system because my hands were shaking so bad, I don't think I could have dialed 911 if I wanted to.

When he answered the phone, I just broke down in tears. I was a mess, and I didn't know what to do. After talking to Devin for a while, I managed to calm down enough to drive home. He told me he would meet me there, and sure enough, when I turned onto my street, his car was parked in the driveway.

When I got out of the car, I ran straight into his arms and began sobbing again.

"It's going to be okay," he said, kissing me on the forehead.

I was afraid, and I could no longer keep it together. Devin gently took the paper from my hand and looked at it. His cheekbones twitched as they always did when he was angry. He called one of his friends on the police force to file a report.

After the officer left and I was relaxed. Devin called Destini and put her on speaker. He told her about the note, well, about the part where my throat was cut and 'Soon Babe' being written in blood. He suggested that I stay with them for a little while until things settled, or the guy was caught, whichever came first. I could sense Destini's hesitation. She did agree, but I quickly turned down the offer because I wouldn't feel right being in their home, knowing Devin and I were having an affair.

Something was off with Destini, and I couldn't quite put my finger on it. I made a mental note to go by and pay her a visit the following day.

Meanwhile, Devin arranged for an officer to stage outside our residence and to follow me throughout the day. I must say, I felt safe knowing someone had eyes on me for my protection.

But, after two weeks of nothing from this guy, no letters or threatening phone calls, the police ended the security detail, and I was back on my own. I will be the first to admit, I was scared as hell to be without security. I knew someone was out to get me, but the million-dollar question was, who?

Part Three:
Game Over

<h1 style="text-align:center">Destini</h1>

I was packing my bags when my phone dinged. It was an alert from the GPS tracker I had put on Devin's phone. I sat on the bed and opened the app. Devin was at Fantasy, so I clicked on the cameras to see what was going on. At first, everything seemed fine until I clicked in Chloe's room. She was sitting on the bed while he stood in front of her with his wood in her mouth. I turned the camera off in disdain. I had long gotten over their rendezvous. Seeing the two of them didn't affect me like it used to.

"Hello." The voice on the other end of the line was deep and grasp.

"Make it happen tonight." I hung up the phone.

Once I was done packing, I checked the GPS and saw that Devin had left Fantasy.

I tried calling him, but he didn't answer, so I left a message on his voice mail.

"Devin, I have to leave for a few days. I will call you later and explain everything. I love you. Bye."

After leaving Devin a text, I called Chloe.

"Hello," she answered.

"Hey, sis, what's up?"

"Oh, nothing. I'm just doing homework. I'm glad you called. I could use the break."

"Well, good, I'm glad I could help." I teased. "I was calling to ask you a favor."

"Okay, what you need?"

"My cousin Autumn will be here in two days. Will you pick her up from the airport for me? I'm going to visit an old friend and will be gone a couple of days."

"Sure, no problem."

"Thanks, Chloe, love you to the moon and back," I said before ending the call.

Twenty minutes later, I was pulling up to the Four Seasons Hotel. I had planned to enjoy the next five days of luxury, pampering and relaxing, but before I got started, I had some unfinished business to take care of, so I made a call.

"Hello," the female answered.

"Hey, what's the status of the baby?"

"Ms., we are working on it."

"I don't want to hear you're working on it. I want to see results," I yelled and then hit the phone's end button.

She had struck a nerve. For two weeks, I had been back and forth with her and still no baby.

I grabbed my purse off the bed and headed for the bar downstairs. I needed a drink, and I needed one fast.

Devin

estini's car wasn't in the drive when I got home, so I gave her a call.

"Hello," she answered.

Something about her tone sounded off. If I didn't know any better, I would have sworn she was drunk.

"Hey, where you at?"

"I'm at Jeanette's."

"Why are you there, and why didn't you tell me you were going?"

"What are you talking about? I left you a message on your voice mail."

"Oh, is that what you call a message? You didn't tell me where you were going, why you were going, or how long you were going to be there." I snapped.

"Devin, Jeanette is having a crisis, and she needs me. We will talk about this when I get home."

"No, we will talk about this now."

"I'm not going to do this with you. It's not a good time. I will call you tomorrow." She hung up the phone.

I tried calling her back, but she didn't answer. She sent me a text. **"I will be home in a few days. We will talk then."**

I threw the phone on the bed, took off my uniform, and hopped in the shower.

After I was showered and dressed, I called Chloe.

"What are you doing?" I said soon as she answered the phone.

"I'm watching television."

"Pack a bag. I'll be there in thirty minutes."

"Devin, wha-"

"No questions. Just be ready." I ended the call.

I pulled up in front of the house and called Chloe. She picked up on the first ring.

"Hello."

"I'm outside."

"Okay, I'm coming down."

As she walked to the car, it took all I had to not get out of the car and take her right there.

"Devin, what's wrong?" She asked, with concern in her voice.

"I'm fine. Just a little irritated." I started the engine and put the car in gear.

Chloe touched my thigh, and my shaft throbbed.

"Do you want to talk about it?"

I pulled off the curb. "Not right now."

The ride was pretty quiet. I would look over at Chloe from time to time, and I could sense the wheels turning in her head. She wanted to ask questions, but what I loved about her most was her ability to give me space, letting me talk about things when I was ready to talk about them.

When we got off at my exit, she asked. "Why are we getting off on your exit?"

I didn't respond. Shortly thereafter, we were pulling into my driveway.

"Why are we here?" She asked.

I got out of the car and grabbed her bag from the back seat. I went around to the passenger side and opened the door, but she didn't move.

"Devin, tell me now, or you can take me home." She gave me that 'I'm not playing with you' look.

"Destini isn't here, come on, we'll talk about it once we are inside," I said, extending my hand to help her.

She pushed my hand out of the way, getting out of the car on her own.

Once inside, I threw her bag on the couch and pulled her into my arms. I kissed her, gently, at first, then more passionately as the fire rose within my loins.

I slowly walked her back to my bedroom, never breaking our kiss, but she did, long enough to contest having sex in the bed I share with Destini. But I was not hearing it. I picked her up and laid her on the bed. I lifted her dress and pulled her panties down, putting my head between her thighs, and stroking her honey spot with my tongue.

"Mhmm," she moaned.

Gripping the back of my head, she started moving her hips with each stroke of my tongue until she climaxed, causing her entire body to tremble.

I turned her onto her stomach and entered her pulsing hole from behind. She gasped, then taking a breath, she relaxed and clutched my rod. I slid in and out of her wet essences slowly at first, then more rapidly. I thrust deeper and deeper inside of her as the fire inside of me continuously build until I erupted like a volcano releasing hot lava all over her sweet walls.

Chloe

I had just awakened from a wonderful night of sleep when my cell phone dinged. I reached over and grabbed it off the nightstand next to the bed.

It was a message from Destini. She had sent me Autumn's flight schedule.

Autumn was scheduled to arrive at six o'clock that evening, which was perfect, because it gave me plenty of time to finish my shift at Fantasy, before having to pick her up.

After taking a quick shower and getting dressed, I went downstairs to the call room to relieve Jeff.

"So how is it going? I asked.

Jeff had worked the night shift, and by the way, he looked, it had been a long night.

"I am so glad to see you. I'm ready to get in my bed."

He stood, and I sat down at the desk. I picked up the remote to change the channel on the television.

"Bye," he said, as he turned to leave.

"Sleep tight."

"I will." He nodded. "Call me if you need me."

Four hours into my shift, I decided to check the cameras. Devin had given me the passcode due to the last events that had taken place. Just as the cameras appeared on the phone, I noticed a tall man walking out of the yard. I rewound the footage, and there were about ten minutes of footage missing. I immediately called Devin to let him know.

"Hey, check the camera footage," I said. My voice was a little shaken.

"Did you see something?"

"Yes, a guy walking away from the house."

"I'm pulling it up now. Any idea who it could be?"

"No."

"Well, let's see here."

After carefully examining the footage, he came over to the house to look around just to make sure nothing was tampered with.

"Everything looks fine," he said. "Maybe he was here to see Anna."

"What makes you think he was here to see Anna?"

"Well, one of the guys I had watching the house told me there were a lot of men coming and going from here. He said Anna leaves with them, and a few hours later, they bring her back."

"So, what are you trying to say?"

"Do you really need me to spell it out for you, Chloe?" He gave me this 'don't play stupid' look.

"Well, Anna isn't here right now, so why would he be showing up? And how do you explain the ten minutes of footage missing?"

"Chloe, I don't know. It may be a glitch in the system. I would have to check that out later. But for now, all appears okay."

He walked to his car, and I followed him. He opened his car door and kissed me. "I'll call you later."

Fifteen minutes before my shift was over, Anna called.

"Hi, Chloe." Her chipper voice sounded somewhat annoying.

"Hey, Anna," I said hesitantly. I couldn't wait to hear what excuse she had for going to be late. This was her M-O.

"Will you transfer the lines to my phone?

I 'm not going to be back by the start of my shift."

"Sure, I can do that."

I was just happy she didn't need me to cover her shift.

"Okay, thanks. By the way, can I borrow your car for a little while today? I need to pick up the boxes of fabric for the table décor, and my car is too small."

I could agree with her on that because she drove a small two-door Honda.

"Sure, but I have to pick Autumn up from the airport at six. So, we need to exchange cars before then."

"Okay, I can be there by five."

"Sounds good, oh, and Anna, I need to talk to you."

"About what?"

"It can wait. See you at five."

"Hey, Chloe," Autumn said, giving me a hug. "Thanks for picking me up."

"You're welcome." I returned the hug.

I met Autumn a year ago when she came to visit for two weeks during her summer break. She's still beautiful, with her long wavy hair. Her body is small-framed, but she has all the right curves. What I like about her most is that even though she is beautiful, she doesn't let that go to her head.

"So, Autumn, how long are you going to be here?"

"About a month."

"Awesome, I thought it would be great to throw Destini a baby shower, while you were here, that way she will have some family to attend."

"Baby shower." Autumn had a surprised look on her face.

"Yes," I said, surprised by her reaction. "Didn't you know?"

"No, I didn't know. And I don't understand why Destini didn't tell me she was getting a baby."

"She's not getting a baby; she's having a baby."

She stared at me with this bewildered look on her face.

"Why are you looking at me like that?"

"You don't know, do you?"

"I don't know what?"

She turned her head and looked out the window. "I think Destini should be the one to tell you."

"Tell me what?" I asked, hoping she would tell me something, anything.

"I'm sorry, Chloe, I can't say. It's not my business to tell."

I took a deep breath. It was apparent Autumn wasn't going to answer the question, so I changed the subject.

"Are you hungry?"

"Not really. I'm more sleepy than hungry, but if you want to get a bite to eat, it's cool."

"Let's just grab something and take it back to the house."

"That will work," she smiled.

The rest of our commute home was spent catching up on what's been going on since we last saw each other. I told her all about Fantasy and how Destini was going to pass it on to me because Devin no longer wanted her to work after the baby.

We talked about her discovering her birth mother and the regrets she felt for not reaching out to her before she passed away.

When we arrived home, Autumn settled in Destini's old room, and I went to my room to call Devin.

The person you are trying to dial is not taking phone calls at this time.

After hanging up the phone. I noticed the red light on the house line flashing. I pushed the message button.

Hello. This is Ava Lynn with the Los Angeles Police Department. This message is for Chloe Miller. Please give me a call at 555-4321 as soon as you get this message.

I retrieved the notepad and pen out of the small drawer next to my bed and hit replay. I wrote down the phone number, but before I could place the call, there was a knock at my door.

"Hey, where do you keep the towels and washcloths?" Autumn asked.

"They are in the hall closet to your right." I pointed in the direction of the closet.

"Ok, thanks."

I went back to the task at hand.

"Hello, this is the LA Police department, how may I help you?" The lady answered.

"Hi, I'm Chloe Miller? I received a call from Ava Lynn earlier, and I'm returning the call.

"One moment, please," she said, before placing me on hold.

A few minutes past then, the familiar voice on the answering machine appeared at the end of the line.

"Hello Chloe, this is Ava Lynn, thanks for returning my call."

"What is this about?"

She cleared her throat. "The reason I'm calling is to inform you that your vehicle was involved in an accident and the."

"Whoa, wait a minute. Did you say my vehicle was in an accident?" I asked, making sure I heard her correctly.

"Yes, ma'am, and the officer wanted to know if you knew where your vehicle was?"

"Well, I let my roommate borrow it earlier. Is she alright?"

"Hold on, please."

After what seemed like forever, although I know it was only a couple of minutes, she returned to the phone. "Ms. Chloe, sorry about that, I'm not sure what her condition is, but she was transported to the hospital. Officer Stacks responded to the accident and is requesting that you meet with her in the ER."

"Okay, I'm on my way."

I grabbed my keys and purse off the bed and headed down the hallway. I knocked on Autumn's bedroom door.

"Come in."

"Hey. Anna has been involved in an accident, and I have to get to the hospital. I will be back as soon as I can," I said, closing the door.

"Wait! I'm going with you." Autumn gathered her sneakers from the side of the bed and put them on.

When we got downstairs, I opened the door, and Ty was standing there.

"I was just about to knock," he said.

"No need, come with me," I said, grabbing his arm and continued towards the car.

He snatched away. "What's going on?"

I stopped in my tracks and turned to look at him. "Anna's been in an accident,"

"In an accident, is she alright?"

"Ty, I don't know, but we were told to go to the ER, so that's where we're headed."

"I'm driving," he said, walking past me. I handed him the keys and went to the passenger side of the car.

"Well, what did they say?" He asked as he backed out of the driveway.

"They didn't say much. I told you what they told me."

"Okay, so who was she with?"

"Ty, I don't know. All they told me was she was in the hospital."

I felt my blood pressure rising. Ty was getting on my nerves with his questions. It was bad enough that Anna was in an accident. Who she was with was of no concern to me. I just prayed she was okay.

"Chloe, have you called Destini?"

"No, Autumn, I haven't called her."

"I'll call her."

She took her cell phone out of her pocket.

"Thank you."

"She is not answering," Autumn announced as she put her phone away.

"Okay, we can try later."

I placed my head back on the headrest and closed my eyes. I could feel a migraine coming.

Ty pulled into the ER parking lot. I had opened the car door and was out of the vehicle before he could shut off the engine. He and Autumn got out of the car and trailed behind me.

Once inside, Officer Stacks wasn't hard to find. She was talking with hospital security at the security desk. I approached the counter.

"Hello, Officer Stacks, I'm Chloe Miller. I was told to meet you here," I said when I approached the counter.

"Oh, yes." She looked at Autumn and Ty, who was now standing next to me.

I pointed at Autumn. "This is a friend of ours." Then Ty. "And this is Anna's boyfriend."

She nodded. "Come with me."

She walked us back to the security office.

"Okay, this will give us some privacy," she said, closing the door behind us. "I would first like to ease your minds by letting you know that Anna is going to be okay. The doctors say she will fully recover." The three of us let out a sigh of relief.

"What kind of injuries does she have?" Ty asked.

"She has a broken collar bone, her left leg is broken, and she has a few cracked ribs. She was very fortunate. Right now, she is in surgery. So, the Doctor will give you an update when they're done."

"What caused the accident?" I asked.

"We're not sure; there was no other vehicle involved. As of right now, it seems like Anna ran off the road and hit a tree. Our investigation unit is working the scene as we speak, so hopefully, we will have some answers later on today or at least within a couple of days." She placed her hand on the door handle. "Is there anything else I can help you with?"

"I have a question." Ty stood to get ready to leave.

"Yes."

"Was she by herself?" He asked.

"Yes, she was by herself." Officer Stacks answered.

"Uh, just stupid," I uttered under my breath.

Autumn and I stood up, and Officer Stacks escorted us back to the lobby.

"Someone will come to get you when she's out of surgery," she smiled and walked away.

Destini

"It's done."

"Alright." I smiled.

"Meet me at the Pic and Save parking lot, nine o'clock tonight."

"See you there."

I looked under the bed and pulled the black bag from under it. After recounting the money, I smiled at the five-grand. My cell phone rang again. Instead of answering it, I looked at the caller ID. I had two missed calls from Autumn, and two missed calls from Devin.

I already knew what they were calling me about, so I didn't bother to call them back. I would just wait to talk to them when I got home.

I packed my bags and laid on the bed with a big grin spread across my face. It's done. I replayed the message over and over in my head. Oh, what sweet words they were; *It's done* was like music to my ears until I listened to the voice messages left by Autumn.

Message one: Destini, we are on our way to the hospital. Anna has been in a bad accident. Message two: Destini, Anna, is in surgery. They say she will be alright, but she will have a long road to recovery. Call me as soon as you get this message.

What the hell! I yelled. Shocked by the news, I called Devin.

"Hey, it's me. I got a message from Autumn saying Anna was in an accident. How is she?" I managed to say in one breath.

"She's banged up pretty bad, but she will be okay. Why haven't you been answering your phone?"

"My phone died, and it was on the charger."

"You've been letting your phone die a lot here lately," he said sarcastically.

I ignored him. "So, how did the accident happen?"

"Don't know yet. Anna was driving Chloe's car. We are going to have someone from the crime unit look at it."

"Was anyone in the car with her?"

"No, there wasn't."

"Oh, my goodness. I'm so happy she's going to be alright."

"Yeah, me, too."

"Well, I'll call you later." I ended the call.

Devin called me right back, but I didn't answer, I had to make a call, fast.

"Yeah."

"It's not done."

"What do you mean it's not done?"

"Wrong one."

"Wrong one?"

"Yep."

"How is that? I did what you told me."

"You got the right pond, but the wrong fish."

"Well, I had no control over that."

"I know you didn't, but if you want to get paid, you will complete the job."

"I see. Well, unless you want to become extinct. You better pay me my money."

"Like I said. When the job is finished, I will pay you. I'm not paying for a half-ass job! Don't call me until you get it done." I pushed the end button on the phone.

After packing my things, I called Autumn to let her know I was on my way.

Devin

I arrived at the hospital and found Chloe and another young lady sitting in the lobby.

"Hey," I said, bending down to give Chloe a hug. "How is she?" I sat next to her and placed my arm around her shoulders.

"Officer Stacks said the doctors told her Anna was going to fully recover, but we haven't seen the doctor yet."

The young lady sitting on the other side of Chloe watched me closely.

"Oh, Devin, this is Autumn-Destini's cousin. Autumn, Devin."

I removed my arm from around Chloe's shoulders.

"Hello," I said.

We exchanged a handshake.

"Hi, so you are the infamous Devin. I've heard a lot about you," she smiled.

"All good, I hope."

"Hmm, well…" She had a pensive look on her face. "Naw, I'm just kidding, of course, it was all good."

The three of us laughed.

"Destini is on her way," Chloe said, once the laughter subsided.

"Yeah, I know." I lied. I didn't know, but I was happy to hear it. "Excuse me. I need to make a call."

I returned to the lobby and sat across from both ladies. "Did the doctor tell the officer how long, Anna was going to be in surgery?" I asked.

"No, she didn't." Chloe sighed. "Devin, have you seen my car?"

"Yes, I have."

"Well, how bad is it?"

"I'm sorry, Chloe, but it's totaled."

She gasped and covered her mouth with her hand. "Oh, no!" She shook her head.

"You will need to call your insurance company in the morning."

She nodded. "I will."

An hour and a half had passed before we were able to see Anna. When we got to her room, Ty was already there by her side. Anna was lying there, partially in a daze.

I said hello and sat down on the small couch in front of her bed.

Chloe and Autumn didn't waste any time hovering over her. Ty moved out of their way and joined me.

"Hey man, how you holding up?" I asked as we bumped fist.

"I'm good."

We both watched the ladies as they did all they could to make Anna comfortable.

We were with Anna for about two hours before Destini showed up. When she walked into the room, she went straight to Anna's bedside. I couldn't help but notice the surprised look on Autumn's face when she laid eyes on Destini's belly.

"Hey, Anna," she said with tears in her eyes. She gently stroked the top of Anna's head.

Anna opened her eyes. "Hey," she said with a weak smile.

"I got here as fast as I could. I'm so happy you are going to be okay."

"Me, too." Anna closed her eyes.

"She's still groggy from the anesthesia," Chloe said.

Destini nodded and walked over to Autumn.

She gave Autumn a hug. "Hey cousin, I'm so happy to see you." She whispered in Autumn's ear, and released her from her embrace.

I wondered what that was about. Whatever it was, the look on Autumn's face showed her discontentment.

Destini walked over to the couch and sat down between Ty and me.

"Hey, you." She leaned in to give me a kiss, but I moved my head so that her kiss landed on my cheek. I wanted her to know that all was not forgiven, and we would be talking about it later. Suddenly, there was a knock at the door. Then it was pushed open.

First to enter was DEA agent Fulton and behind him was LAPD Officer Pilgrim. Agent Fulton walked over to Destini.

"Destini Johnson, you are under arrest for the attempted murder of Chloe Miller, anything you say can and will be used against you," He grabbed her by the arm, and she tried to wrestle from his grip.

"I haven't done anything, you piece of shit, let me go," she shouted. "You are the one who tampered with her car, not me."

Chloe stood with her mouth agape. Autumn and Ty were both just as stunned. Anna opened her eyes to witness the madness as it unfolded.

"Devin, you're just going to stand there and let him treat me like this? I'm your wife," she pleaded, but I didn't move.

Agent Fulton tried to handcuff her other arm. "Ma'am, stop resisting arrest."

Destini wouldn't comply, so Officer Pilgrim stepped in to assist him.

Chloe held her hand up. "Wait! Don't you see she's pregnant? Stop handling her like that."

"That's right," Destini snapped.

I pulled Chloe back. "There's no baby, Chloe," I said, looking at Destini.

"Yes, there is Devin. I promise you. I'm pregnant."

She started to cry. After the officer handcuffed her, he escorted her out of the room.

"Wait a minute." Chloe stopped the officers. "I have to see it for myself."

She lifted Destini's shirt. There it was, the fake belly bump. Chloe shook her head in disgust. She stepped aside, and the officer proceeded out the door with Destini in tow. Agent Fulton followed behind him, before walking out of the room he turned around.

"I need all of you to come down to the station."

"We will see you there," I said speaking, for everyone.

He nodded and left.

Anna started taking off the bandages.

"What the hell just happened?" Chloe asked, still in disbelief.

"I'm wondering the same thing myself," Ty responded.

Agent Fulton will explain everything when we get to the station. I looked over at Autumn. She looked confused and lost. I touched her on the shoulder.

"It's going to be alright."

"I don't think so. I have to call my Aunt and Uncle." She walked out the door.

"This is some crazy shit right here," Ty said, removing the last of Anna's bandages.

"Tell me about it. I would have never thought Destini would do something like this." Anna replied.

She got up from the bed, and we all left the room.

When we got to the elevators, Autumn was leaning against the wall. She ended her call and joined us on the ride to the first floor.

Once we were outside, Chloe and Autumn rode with me, while Anna and Ty followed us in Anna's car.

"So, how did you know Destini wasn't pregnant?" Chloe asked.

"I found the fake bellies."

"I wonder why she would fake a pregnancy," Chloe stated, not really expecting an answer, but Autumn provided one anyway.

"Destini can't have children. She has always wanted them, though."

Chloe adjusted herself in her seat so that she could look at Autumn, who was sitting behind me in the backseat. Autumn continued.

"Destini was born with MRKH."

"What's that?" Chloe asked.

I looked in the rearview mirror and made eye contact with Autumn. She held her head down and took a moment. I could tell by looking at her that she wasn't sure she should continue. She then cleared her throat and started to speak.

"MRKH stands for Mayer-Rokitansky-Küster-Hauser syndrome. It's when a female is born without, or with an underdeveloped uterus and vagina. In Destini's case, she was born without a uterus."

"Uh, Okay." Chloe turned around in her seat. "I still don't get it. How did she think she was going to get away with all of this?"

"Because she didn't think," I said.

I knew exactly how she thought she was going to get away with it, but I couldn't reveal it to Chloe, not just yet anyway.

Chloe

When those officers came into Anna's hospital room and arrested Destini for attempting to murder me, I didn't know what to think. It saddened me that my BFF wanted me dead. What did I ever do to her? I asked myself that question a thousand times.

Sure, I continued to see Devin, but he was mine first. If anything, I should've been the one mad. Then there's the whole fake pregnancy thing. It was just unbelievable, unreal as if someone was playing a cruel joke.

When we got down to the police station, an officer was escorting Jeff to the back, in handcuffs.

"Jeff," I called out. He stopped and looked at me, then held his head down. The officer nudged him to continue walking.

I looked at Devin. "What did he do?"

"It will all be explained to you in a little bit, just be patient," he said and disappeared behind the security door.

The rest of us sat quietly in the lobby. Eventually, we were called one by one—first Ty, then Anna, Autumn, and lastly, me.

When I walked into the interview room, I noticed right away, the plain white walls with cameras positioned in each corner of the room. There was a round brown table with a faux green plant placed at the center of the table, and it was surrounded by six blue leather chairs.

I sat at the table, across from Devin, Agent Fulton, and another man who was identified as Investigator Rubin.

"Hello, Chloe. I'm Rubin Stills." He held out his hand. "I'm the investigator working this case."

I nodded, and we exchanged a handshake.

"Chloe, do you know why Mrs. Johnson would try to harm you?" He asked.

"No, I don't. Destini's my best friend, and we didn't have any problems, at least none that I knew of."

He nodded his head. "I see. Well, I'm sure you'd want to know how all of this came about, so I'm not going to delay it any longer."

He told me how Destini had placed a hidden camera in the ceiling fan in my bedroom right after her honeymoon so, she knew Devin, and I was having an affair. She conspired with Jeff at first. Their plan was to scare me enough to make me want to leave school and go back home, by way of phone calls and the photo on my car.

When that didn't work, she hired Agent Fulton, not knowing he was an undercover DEA agent. He contacted LAPD, and they started a sting operation.

Agent Fulton and Officer Rye, who was also under-cover, first contact with Destini was at the movie theater. Destini had left behind the first down payment of twenty-five hundred dollars for him in the Five Heartbeats theater room- Row six, Seat nine, hence the 69ers.

Officer Rye recognized Destini from her comings and goings from Fantasy. Unknown to me, Devin had already gotten the ball rolling with LAPD Officer Rye and Officer Woods, who were our neighbors. They were the ones who moved into the vacant house across the street. Investigator Rubin went on to explain that today was the day I was supposed to die. That was a hard pill to swallow.

When I left to pick Autumn up from the airport, Officer Woods walked across the street and knocked on the door. When Anna answered, he took her back to his place, and he and Officer Rye explained every-thing to her. Anna was told to drive my car to the alleged accident site. They had a vehicle that was a replica of mine already there. They put make-up on

Anna and staged the accident. They even had the ambulance to transport Anna to the hospital. They had thought of everything. But what they didn't count on was Destini not meeting up with Agent Fulton to pay him his final payment. That was where they were initially going to apprehend her.

So, when Destini called Autumn and told her, she was on the way, that was a huge bonus because they knew she would have no escape.

When Devin left the lobby to make his phone call, he called Investigator Rubin to let him know Destini was on her way, and the rest is history, so to speak.

I sat speechless as I processed every word he said.

Devin waved his hand to get my attention.

"Chloe, are you alright?"

It wasn't until he stood up from the table that I snapped out of my trance.

"I want to go home."

"Is it ok for me to take her home?" Devin asked.

"Sure, I will give her a call if I have any more questions." He stood. "Ms. Miller, I'm sorry you've had to go through all of this. You get some rest." He shook my hand and opened the door for us to leave.

Destini

"Hey, are you okay?" Autumn asked. I gave her that 'what do you think' look. "Do I look okay, Autumn? I mean, look at me, I'm behind freaking bars!" I said, annoyed and pissed at her for asking such a stupid ass question. Really, who in the hell asks someone if they're okay when they are in jail as if you are on vacation or something.

"Well, you don't have to bite my head off," she snapped. "I was only asking because I care about you."

I took a deep breath. "I'm sorry, I know you were just being concerned."

I knew it wasn't her fault I was in jail, and she didn't deserve the attitude I was giving her.

"Autumn, I don't know what I'm going to do?"

"I hear you. This is pretty bad, Destini, but I talked to your mom and dad, and they are on their way."

"No, Autumn." I groaned. "why would you do that?" I put my head in my hands.

My parents were the last ones I wanted to know about this, at least until I was ready to tell them myself.

She looked confused. "Why don't you want them to know?"

I shook my head. "It doesn't matter now. It's already done. Where's Devin?" I asked, changing the subject.

"I think he's gone. I saw him and Chloe leaving before they called me back to see you. What's up with them anyway?"

"Autumn, it's a long story. I will tell you about it when I get out of here."

I was furious to hear that Devin had left with Chloe. I was his wife, but he never gave me a chance to show him how good life could be with me. I tried everything I could to get him to love me. But all that got me was here, behind bars.

"Time's up," the jailer announced.

"Okay, well, I'm going to hang around until your parents get here," Autumn said as she stood to leave.

I nodded. "Hey, don't mention Fantasy to my parents, okay?"

"Okay."

I could tell she had more questions. Thank God her time was up.

As I sat in my holding cell, I had so many emotions. I was sad, hurt, disappointed, afraid, and, most of all, lost.

I was sad that I had lost my best friend. Chloe had never done anything to me but be there through thick and thin. I'm the one who betrayed her.

I was hurt that Devin didn't stand by me, but who was I kidding? He never loved me. His heart was always with Chloe. If it wasn't for the lie about the pregnancy, he would have never been with me.

I am disappointed in myself. I really can't believe I was willing to kill the one person that showed me nothing but love, even though I didn't deserve it. I know I have to pay for my actions, and that scares me. However, at this time, it's my parents that I fear most.

My dad is the honorable Judge Riviera. He is loving but hard. My mother; she's the opposite; she's caring and kind. They raised me to be better than this. The thought of seeing the hurt and disappointment in their eyes breaks my heart. All I can do now is ask the people I hurt for forgiveness and hope that one day, they would be able to forgive me.

Devin

Chloe gazed out of the window as I drove her home. I took her hand and gently squeezed it. She turned to look at me.

"How did you know she wasn't pregnant?"

"I told you, I found the baby bumps."

"Baby bumps?"

Chloe was not acting like herself. She had already asked me that question earlier.

"Yes, fake pregnant bellies? Remember, I told you I had found them. And you saw the one she had on while we were at the hospital." I nodded.

"Oh yeah. Where were they again?"

"They were in the trunk she kept in her closet."

She nodded and rested her head on the seat.

"I'm still trying to figure out how she thought she was going to get away with all of this? I mean, she couldn't pretend to be pregnant forever."

"She was going to buy a baby."

"You mean like purchase a baby on the black market?"

"Yep."

"OMG! That's Crazy!"

"I know. It's still hard for me to believe that Destini would actually go that far."

She shook her head. "How did you find that out?"

"I overheard her on the telephone telling someone that she needed it done quick, and that made me suspicious. So, while she was gone her trip, I did some snooping around and found the baby bumps.

The next day I went to the phone company and got a copy of her phone records. I called the phone numbers that were around the time I overheard her call. The first number I called a female answered, but when I started questioning her, she hung up. I noticed there were several calls made to that particular phone number, so I contacted Robert, and he did some research of his own. The lady was involved in a baby black market ring."

"Wow! Unbelievable."

"Yep." I pulled into the driveway. "I can stay if you like," I said, turning to face her.

"No, I'm good. I need some time to figure all of this out." She unfastened her seatbelt.

I understood her needing time alone. It was a lot for anyone to have to deal with.

I kissed her on the forehead. "I'll call you later."

Truth is, I needed to be alone to process all of this myself. As I drove home, I thought about everything that had happened. I knew there were a lot of uncertainties, but one thing I knew for sure; it was over between Destini and me. I smiled as the thought of me being free to be with Chloe crossed my mind. She is the love of my life, and I wouldn't have it any other way.

Epilogue

Chloe

The following morning, I found out Destini's father is a Judge, and he had brought one of California's prestigious lawyers with them to represent her.

After posting bail, Destini moved back home with her parents on the premise of them giving the assurance that she would be present for court.

Autumn agreed to take over Fantasy for Destini while she got through all her legalities.

Devin is still working for the LA Police Department. He has filed for an annulment, which should be finalized in a couple of weeks. Surprisingly, Destini is being cooperative.

As for me, I left Fantasy at the request of Autumn and moved in with Devin. We are planning to get married next summer. Until then, we are happily in love and treasure every moment we share together.